MAXi MEETS THE JUGGLERS

WRITTEN BY THOMAS MINTON
ILLUSTRATED BY TODD DAKINS

One of Four Stories
in The Adventures of Taxi Dog Series

see-saw

publishing

Text by Thomas Minton • Illustrations by Todd Dakins

Book design by Noble Pursuits LLC with art direction by Elaine Noble

www.maximeetsthejugglers.com • www.peekaboopublishing.com

See-Saw Publishing
Part of the Peek-A-Boo Publishing Group

FIrst Edition 2017 • Printed by Shenzhen TianHong Printing Co., Ltd. in Shenzhen, China

ISBN: 978-1-943154-91-3 (Hardback)
ISBN: 978-1-943154-90-6 (Paperback)

10 9 8 7 6 5 4 3 2 1

PEEK - A - BOO
PUBLISHING GROUP

"Look what I have, Maxi," says Jim.
"Deli sandwiches to go."

"Woof, woof."

"Roast beef, hot dogs, sausage, and blue cheese for you; turkey, bologna, salami, and Swiss cheese for me.

"Rruff," says Maxi nosing ahead.

" Oh, oh! Sorry, Maxi, we will have
to eat our sandwiches later."

Jim hurriedly stuffs the food sack into Maxi's
special glove box as a woman in a striped costume
and clown makeup gets into the taxi.

"Here, I need to get to this address by two o'clock," says the woman.

"Are you a clown?" says Jim.

"My name's Esmeralda and I'm a street performer."

Maxi pops a head over the seat.

"A juggler to be exact."

The juggler tosses three balls in the air and goes through a routine.

"Wow," says Jim, "you're really good at juggling.
What do you say, Maxi?"

"Wooooof!"

"So, here we are," says Jim. "Is this where you perform?"

"I've been juggling here for years," says Esmeralda.
"This is my spot."

"Hey! Who said you could work here?"
yells Esmeralda as she drops her bag of striped balls.

"Hey! I didn't see your name on it!"
"I'm Julio the Great and I'm doing my show here today."

Well, I'm Esmeralda the Greatest
and I am the greatest juggler."

"Oh, oh," says Jim.
"Do you smell trouble between these two?"

"Gruff, rruff," says Maxi sniffing the air from the taxi window.

"Maxi to the rescue."
says Jim. "I know you will
be able to get these two
working together. I'll meet
you later after I find a place
to park the taxi."

"Rruff."

"Juggling balls is all about balance," says Esmeralda, juggling many balls.

"Well, I juggle pins and juggling pins is all about rhythm," says Julio.

"Murph," sighs Maxi.

"Who's that?" asks Julio pointing to Maxi.

"That's Maxi the Taxi Dog," says Esmeralda, "who's part of my act."

"Is that so?" says Julio. "Let's see how Maxi balances a pin."

He tosses a pin to Maxi who juggles it before balancing perfectly.
"Aha! Now Maxi's part of **MY** act."

Maxi spins the pin back
to Julio while balancing a
striped ball from Esmeralda
on an open paw.

"Grrrr!" says Maxi.

"Hey, this is fun!" says Julio.

"I agree," says Esmeralda, "we make a good team."

"All because of Maxi," says Julio.

"Good work, Maxi," says Jim, "C'mon, let's eat our sandwiches."
"Woof!"

"All the meat and cheese got juggled together in the bag,
so I guess if you can eat my turkey and bologna and Swiss cheese,
I can eat your roast beef, hot dogs, sausage and blue cheese. "

"Rruff!"

The End